2·9

D0872037

PONY ♡ GIRLS
Daniela

By Lisa Mullarkey
Illustrated by Paula Franco

Calico

An Imprint of Magic Wagon
abdopublishing.com

To Haritha, Jane, and Brittany: Way more than colleagues.
Family! —LM

To my family, for teaching me to follow my dreams. —PF

abdopublishing.com

Published by Magic Wagon, a division of ABDO, PO Box 398166, Minneapolis, Minnesota 55439. Copyright © 2016 by Abdo Consulting Group, Inc. International copyrights reserved in all countries. No part of this book may be reproduced in any form without written permission from the publisher. Calico™ is a trademark and logo of Magic Wagon.

Printed in the United States of America, North Mankato, Minnesota.
092015
012016

Written by Lisa Mullarkey
Illustrated by Paula Franco
Edited by Heidi M.D. Elston, Megan M. Gunderson & Bridget O'Brien
Designed by Jillian O'Brien
Art Direction by Candice Keimig

Library of Congress Cataloging-in-Publication Data

Mullarkey, Lisa, author.
  Daniela / by Lisa Mullarkey ; illustrated by Paula Franco.
    pages cm. -- (Pony Girls)
  Summary: In her first year at Storm Cliff Stables horse camp Daniela Cruz is having a hard time fitting in, partly because her cousin Gabriela seems to be so much better at everything to do with riding than she is--but Dani is a superior swimmer, a talent that could save the day if she can find the special ring that Aunt Jane lost in the lake.
  ISBN 978-1-62402-128-2
1. Riding schools--Juvenile fiction. 2. Camps--Juvenile fiction. 3. Cousins--Juvenile fiction. 4. Horses--Juvenile fiction. 5. Friendship--Juvenile fiction. 6. Self-confidence--Juvenile fiction. [1. Camps--Fiction. 2. Cousins--Fiction. 3. Horses--Fiction. 4. Friendship--Fiction. 5. Self-confidence--Fiction. 6. Costa Rican Americans--Fiction.] I. Franco, Paula, illustrator. II. Title.
  PZ7.M91148Dan 2016
  813.6
  [Fic 2 23]
                    2015023275

Table of Contents

"Whatcha doin' Aunt Jane?" I asked.

The stable was quiet. The horses were out in the pasture.

She swooshed a pitchfork through a pile of hay. "Mucking out Queenie's stall. It's extra messy today. Looks like the horses had a party."

Aunt Jane isn't my real aunt. She owns Storm Cliff Stables. The best camp around! Everyone just calls her Aunt Jane.

"Can we help?" I asked her.

"That's sweet of you to ask, Dani."

Kianna crossed her fingers. "Pretty please with a cherry on top?"

"Two cherries," said Carly.

Gabriela didn't say anything. Her nose was stuck in a book. Again.

Carly pointed to a wheelbarrow. It was full of stinky manure. "Gross!" She pinched her nose. "Never mind. I don't wanna help."

Kianna pinched her nose, too.

But I just held my breath. I can hold it for over a minute! Around stinky manure, you get a lot of practice.

"A clean stall helps the horses stay healthy," said Aunt Jane. "We try to muck each stall twice a day. We'll teach you Pony Girls soon enough."

Pony Girls are first-year campers. We're eight years old.

Gabriela said, "I know how already." Then she reached for Aunt Jane's hand. "But shouldn't you take off your ring? My mom never wears her rings when she's cleaning."

Gabriela is my cousin. But we barely know each other. She lives in California, thousands of miles from where I live in Costa Rica.

I *thought* we'd be best friends this summer. But now I wasn't so sure.

I wasn't even sure we'd end up being best *cousins*.

Aunt Jane twirled the ring around her finger. "It's my lucky ring. I never take it off. It was my grandmother's." She pressed it against her heart.

Gabriela handed the book to Aunt Jane. "Look at chapter five."

I was pretty sure Gabriela liked books better than me.

Aunt Jane scanned the pages. "How to Muck Stalls. So you do know how."

Great. Is there anything Gabriela can't do?

Aunt Jane glanced at her watch. "I'm done in here." She wiped a drop of sweat off her nose and plopped down on a hay bale. "And I'm plum tuckered out. I need a vacation."

I let out my breath. One minute twenty-three seconds! "A vacation?" I said. "I know where you should go!"

Aunt Jane scratched her head. "Hmmm...let me guess." She tapped her foot. "Could it be...Costa Rica?"

"How did you know?" I asked.

Gabriela rolled her eyes. "Because that's all you talk about."

"Is not," I said.

"Is too," she said.

I gave her my cranky eyes. "The rain forest is the most beautiful place on earth, Aunt Jane! I've seen toucans, jaguars, and anteaters. There's a Cloud Forest Reserve in Costa Rica, too! It rains over 100 inches a year. And if you visit, you'll see lots of hummingbirds."

"I saw one once," said Carly. "It looked like a bee. My brother tried to squash it."

Kianna crinkled her nose. "That's mean. My mama loves hummingbirds."

Carly shrugged. "He's only two. He's not smart yet. My mom calls him Monkey Boy."

"Then he would love Costa Rica, too," I said. "There are monkeys everywhere."

"Tell Aunt Jane about the butterflies," said Kianna.

"Butterflies are my very most favorite thing in this world," I said. I glanced at her ring. "I bet I love them as much as you love your lucky ring."

Aunt Jane laughed. "Wow! You must love butterflies to the moon and back then."

I flapped my arms and fluttered around the stable. "There are over a thousand kinds of butterflies there. My favorite is the glasswing. Besides a dark outline around its wings, the rest of it looks like glass. You can see right through the wings!" I stopped fluttering. "My abuela says I've probably seen most of them!"

"Most of them?" asked Gabriela. "I've seen all of them."

"That's impossible," I said. *At least I thought it was impossible.* "But at the Butterfly Conservatory, all different butterflies land on you. I've had so many land on me that Abuela calls me the Butterfly Queen."

Carly pointed to Gabriela. "What does she call you?"

Gabriela stammered, "I . . . I don't know."

"What? That's weird," said Carly.

"It's not weird," I said. "Abuela won't fly, so they've never met."

Carly gasped. "Why don't you visit her?" she asked Gabriela.

Gabriela shrugged. "My parents are busy with the ranch."

Gabriela's ranch is huge. She owns more horses than Aunt Jane!

Aunt Jane patted her back. "I understand. I don't get away from Storm Cliff much. There's always work to be done." She looked out the window. "Well, look at that!"

"A butterfly!" I said.

"I've had butterfly bushes for years with no luck," said Aunt Jane. "But ever since you've arrived, so have the butterflies."

I stopped flapping and put my finger out in front of my chest. *Please land on me.*

The butterfly danced around Gabriela and then landed on her shoulder.

"It likes you," said Kianna.

Carly giggled. "You're the Butterfly Queen. Shouldn't it land on you?"

Gabriela smirked. "Maybe I should become a lepidopterist."

"A lap-a-what?" I said.

Gabriela shook her head. "It's someone who studies butterflies."

Carly laughed. "Shouldn't the Butterfly Queen know that?"

The other Pony Girls laughed, too.

I wanted to flutter back to my cabin.

Chapter 2

The Sugar Thieves

"Maybe I need help leading some horses into their stalls after all," said Aunt Jane.

Carly did a cartwheel. "We can bring all of them inside!"

"Whoa," said Aunt Jane. "That's a lot of horses! If you each bring in one, that would be helpful. The sooner we get the horses tacked up, the sooner we get out on the trails."

Trail rides are my favorite!

Aunt Jane looked around the stable. "Get Queenie's halter, Gabriela."

Each halter hung on a hook outside the horse's stall.

"Can I get Sapphire's?" asked Carly.

Carly loves Sapphire. She's a chestnut Thoroughbred. She's too big for Carly to ride, so Carly usually walks her around the arena.

"Of course," said Aunt Jane. She scanned the empty stalls. "Kianna, can you get Sunburst's halter?"

"I'll get Blue's," I said.

Aunt Jane frowned. "Sorry, Dani. Blue's stubborn. He'll only allow Layla, Bree, or me to lead him. And Jaelyn, of course."

Jaelyn and Bree are older campers. Layla is our counselor.

Aunt Jane handed me Duke's halter instead. "Ready?"

"Ready," we all said together.

Duke is a black paint gelding with a white blaze. He has two different colored eyes, one blue and one brown!

We trudged out to the pasture. We spotted Queenie first. Aunt Jane gave her a piece of apple. Then she slipped the harness around her head and fastened the lead rope.

"Remember the number one rule when leading a horse or holding onto a rope," said Aunt Jane. "Never ever wrap the rope around your hand. If a horse runs off, it'll drag you."

Gabriela winced. "Once, my dad stood in front of a trailer. The lead rope was wrapped around his hand. When his horse backed down the ramp, it jerked him forward and dragged him down the ramp. The horse was so strong it broke Dad's pinky finger. It's still crooked."

Kianna covered her ears. "Ouch!"

Carly's eyes lit up. "It sounds gross but in a cool kinda way."

Gabriela continued. "My dad taught me how to hold the rope. Can I show them?"

Aunt Jane nodded.

Gabriela always knows what to do. Always.

Gabriela held the rope with her right hand. "Hold the rope with your thumb on top. About six inches from the halter ring like this." She slid her fingers down the rope a bit. "Now fold the rest of the rope and hold it in your other hand so it doesn't drag on the ground."

Gabriela stood next to Queenie. "Don't lead by walking in front of your horse. If the horse gets spooked, it could run you over. Lead by standing next to your horse."

"Impressive," said Aunt Jane.

"Show-off," I whispered.

Then Gabriela stuck out her tongue at me.

Rude, rude, rude!

I wanted to stick out my tongue back, but Aunt Jane was watching. So I held my breath instead. One minute and twenty-four seconds!

Once the horses had their halters on, we led them into the stable. We brushed them while Aunt Jane gave each one a sugar cube.

Finally, she grabbed Blue's harness. "I'll be back."

As soon as she left, Carly grabbed my hand. "I know where Aunt Jane keeps the sugar cubes. Let's get some."

I grabbed Kianna's hand and then she grabbed Gabriela's hand.

But Gabriela wouldn't come with us. "That's stealing."

Carly frowned. "It's just a sugar cube. There are *millions* of them."

Kianna added, "Aunt Jane won't care."

Gabriela kept brushing Queenie. "I don't want one."

But we did. So we followed Carly. We took three cubes each.

When we got back to Queenie's stall, Gabriela wasn't there.

Carly glanced out the window and squinted. "Is that Blue with Aunt Jane and Gabriela?"

Kianna bobbed her head up and down. "Yep! Gabriela's leading Blue! Didn't Aunt Jane say he wouldn't move for just anyone?"

I peered out the window. It was Blue! I bit down on my sugar cube. Didn't they know that Gabriela wasn't just anyone? She was perfect. It was obvious everyone thought so.

Everyone but me.

"Are you sure you don't want to go on a trail ride?" asked Aunt Jane. She twirled her ring around her finger again. "You changed your mind so quickly."

I glared at Gabriela and Blue and nodded. "I'm going to arts and crafts instead. I'll make my picture frame."

"I still need to make mine, too," said Carly. "I'll go with you."

Aunt Jane turned to Kianna and Gabriela. "How about you two?"

They nodded. So while they got their horses ready, Carly and I walked down to the small barn.

Lots of girls were already there.

"Last time, you made horseshoe frames and put a picture of you and your horse inside," said Layla.

When Aunt Jane had told me to say cheese, Duke chortled!

"Today, you're going to decorate a BFF frame. Hundreds of pictures are tacked to the bulletin boards. Grab one. If there isn't one with your BFF, we'll take it today."

"Who's your BFF?" asked Carly. "Kianna's my new best friend, you know."

I nodded.

"Are you putting you and Gabriela in your frame?" she asked.

"I'm not sure," I said. "I guess not?"

"But you're cousins," she said. "You're probably in her frame."

I perked up. "Oh, then I will!"

Maybe my mom was right. Maybe we would end up being BFFs.

We decorated our frames. I used pink buttons. I glued purple sequins on top of them since Gabriela's favorite color is purple. Then I glued plastic butterflies on each corner. They matched my hair clips.

I held it up. "Done."

"Love it," said Layla. "Put it on the bench and let it dry."

We walked over to the bench.

Carly lifted up a blue frame. "Here's Kianna's."

There was a picture of Kianna and Carly sitting on Duke. They were making silly faces. I made a silly face back at the picture.

I studied the rest of the frames. I saw frames with pictures of Bree and Jaelyn, Esha and Avery, and even one of Avery and Aunt Jane.

"Here's Gabriela's," said Carly. "It looks like she bought it in a store."

It sparkled. It was covered with shells and sea glass.

It was perfect. Except for the picture of Kianna, Carly, and Gabriela inside.

Where was I?

I stamped my foot. "Gabriela doesn't like me."

Carly tried to cheer me up. "There probably wasn't a picture of you guys together." She scanned the wall. "I don't see any pictures of you."

But I did. "Look," I said. "Here are two of Gabriela and me on the trail."

Carly scratched her head. "Maybe she *doesn't* like you. What did you do to her?"

"I didn't do anything!" I said. "She's just so . . . Miss Perfect Pants."

"It sounds like *you* don't like *her*."

I stared at all the photos.

Carly patted my back. "That's okay. Sometimes I don't like my brother. He bites, and I wish I could bite back."

"Okay," Carly continued. "Pick your person. Just don't forget that I gave you my ice cream cone last night."

I bit my lip. "But you picked Kianna."

Carly pointed to the frames. "But no one picked you. You need a best friend. If you want, I'll be it."

"You will?" I asked.

She nodded. "If you give me your extra dessert tonight." She flashed a smile. "Just kidding."

A minute later, we got a new picture taken.

"Smile," said Layla.

But how could I smile when I felt so sad?

Chapter 4

Winning Dinner

"Can you braid my hair?" asked Carly.

It was dinnertime.

"Sure," I said.

Gabriela walked over. "Why don't you french braid it?"

Carly's eyes lit up. "I love french braids!"

I shook my head. "Sorry. I know mine look fancy, but they're just regular braids. I don't know how to make a french braid."

"I do," said Gabriela. "Here, let me."

As I watched Gabriela move her fingers through Carly's hair, my face got hot. I didn't want to cry, so I held my breath and timed myself again. One minute twenty-nine seconds!

Kianna was watching, too.

"Want me to braid yours?" I asked.

She shuffled her feet. "Gabriela can do it. I've never had a french braid before."

I glared at Gabriela.

Gabriela said, "I guess if you're the Butterfly Queen, I can be the Braid Queen."

I clenched my fists and stormed right out the door!

Lucky for me, I walked into Avery outside her cabin. She was cleaning her boots.

"Where are you going?" asked Avery. "Dinner hasn't started."

I sniffled.

"Uh-oh. Pony Girl problems?" she asked. "Or do you miss home?"

"Both," I said and sat down.

"But mostly Pony Girl problems. Gabriela does *everything* better than me. I always braid Carly's and Kianna's hair. But now the Braid Queen is making *french* braids."

Avery laughed. "Well, I'm not any kind of queen."

"It's not funny," I said. "I was the Butterfly Queen first. But then a butterfly landed on her, not me."

I wiped my nose. "She's always showing off. When I told her I finally hula-hooped with *three* hoops, she told me she used *four*."

I picked up a pebble and threw it.

"When I ate four s'mores last night, she had to eat five. Then she said she was the S'mores Queen!"

Avery rubbed her stomach. "You're lucky you're not sick!"

"If I did get sick, Gabriela would say she was even sicker."

Avery put down her boot. "She sounds like a one-upper."

"A one-whater?" I said.

"A one-upper," she said again. "Someone who's always trying to do something a little bit better than you. Last year there was a camper who tried to one-up everyone. She wanted to be the best in everything."

"Gabriela doesn't *want* to be the best in everything. She already *is* the best. So what should I do?"

"There's not too much you can do," said Avery. "Did you talk to her about it? Tell her your feelings are hurt. Ask her to stop trying to top you."

"Did that work for you?" I asked.

She shook her head. "Nope. She kept on one-upping me and everyone else. So Esha decided to one-up her."

"Did that work?" I asked.

"Yep. She got the hint," said Avery.

I hugged Avery. "Thanks!"

"Good luck," she said.

Where was Aunt Jane's lucky ring when you needed it? But at dinner, I got my chance to one-up Gabriela.

"We have a special buffet planned for tonight," said Aunt Jane. "A few weeks ago, we asked your families to send us your favorite recipe. One that would make you feel right at home here at Storm Cliff. So tonight, we'll feast on your favorite foods!"

Everyone cheered.

Carly clapped. "I bet they made my mom's meatballs."

"And my mama's lasagna," said Kianna.

Gabriela rubbed her belly. "I hope my mom sent her spare ribs recipe. She won second place in a contest."

"Second place?" I repeated. *This is my chance!* "Abuela's chicken empanadas took first in a contest."

Gabriela frowned.

Layla grabbed the microphone. "We made enough food for everyone to try a little bit of everything. Then you'll vote for your favorite. Whatever wins will be featured during Parents' Day."

Everyone cheered.

Gabriela stood and clapped.

So I stood on my chair and cheered and clapped even louder.

Gabriela puffed out her cheeks and sat down.

I climbed off my chair, too.

One-upping did not make me feel better. One-upping made me feel down.

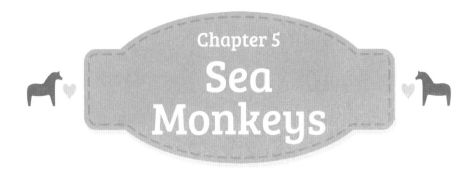

Chapter 5
Sea Monkeys

After breakfast the next day, we voted for our favorite foods.

"Be fair," said Aunt Jane. "Don't vote for your own."

I scanned the ballot and put a check next to Gabriela's spare ribs. Yummy!

Fair and square.

I saw Kianna put an X next to my empanadas.

Then Carly checked the same box!

But when I looked over at Gabriela, a frowny face was next to my name.

Rude, rude, rude! I turned over my pencil and erased my vote.

Then I voted for Avery's pulled pork and handed in my ballot.

A few minutes later, Aunt Jane grabbed the mic. "Campers, we have a winner. This dish will be served along with our special Parents' Day menu. Drum roll, please."

Every camper pounded on the table until Layla held up her hand.

Aunt Jane took a deep breath. "And the winner is . . . Avery Donaldson's pulled pork!"

I ripped my napkin in half.

Carly wrinkled her nose. "Your empanadas should have won."

Kianna agreed. "My mama's gonna want that recipe."

"I'll get it from my abuela," I said. "She says it's a top secret recipe, but I know she'll share it."

Gabriela sucked in her breath. "They looked really good."

I shook my fist in the air. "Then

why didn't you vote for them? I saw your frowny face."

"I couldn't vote for them," she said. "It wouldn't have been fair."

"Why not?" I said.

"Chicken gives me a stomach ache," she said. "That's why I put a frowny face next to it."

I took a deep breath. "So you didn't *not* vote for me just . . . because . . . because you don't like me?"

She didn't get to answer because Aunt Jane came by. "The vote was close, girls. You came in second."

"Really?" I said. "My empanadas?"

"No." She pointed to Gabriela. "Her spare ribs. They were a hit. I might try to convince the cooks to make both dishes for the parents."

Great. One-upped again.

"Gabriela only lost by one vote," said Aunt Jane.

I thought about my erasing. I was the reason she lost.

Not so fair and square after all. I pushed the thought out of my head. "Want to swim before we ride today?"

Swimming always cheers me up.

"Can't," said Carly. "I have vaulting in a few minutes."

"I'll go," said Gabriela.

"Me too," said Kianna.

So the three of us walked to the lake and wriggled out of our clothes. We always have bathing suits on!

Then Kianna ran toward the water. "Last one to the float is a rotten egg!"

Gabriela swam out to the float lickety-split. She was the fastest swimmer. Kianna was second. When I finally got there, they were waving their hands in front of their noses.

"Dani's the rotten egg!" said Kianna.

"Then call me a capuchin monkey! In Costa Rica, I met a white-faced monkey. He snatched eggs right out of my basket. Abuela said he was a rotten, naughty monkey," I said.

"Name-calling is mean. Even for a monkey," said Gabriela.

"Abuela's not mean," I said. "She was kidding."

Gabriela rolled her eyes.

"Now she puts leftover eggs in a basket by the fence. That same monkey comes and steals them every day. He breaks them open with a stone."

"A stone?" said Gabriela. "I don't believe you."

"It's true," I said. "Look it up in one of your books."

Kianna pursed her lips. "My mama would shoo that monkey away." Then Kianna pretended to shoo us away.

For the rest of the morning, we pretended we were monkeys. We played Monkey in the Middle and Monkey See, Monkey Do.

We had more fun than a barrel of monkeys, even though Gabriela kept winning everything.

"Let's play Sea Monkeys," I said. I grabbed the Surf and Turf Dive Rings and threw them in the air.

They landed in the water and sank.

"First one to get a ring is the winner."

I got all four!

"No fair," said Kianna. "We can't hold our breath underwater long enough to find one."

"Let's try again," said Gabriela.

No matter how hard she tried, she never brought a dive ring back up to the surface. I got all four again.

Kianna put one on my head. "You're the Hold Your Breath Queen."

Gabriela panted. "And the Ring Dive Champ!"

Avery swam by. "Looks like you two are having a blast together."

I gave her two thumbs up. Then I crossed my fingers and made a wish.

Please don't let there be any more monkey business.

Chapter 6
A Shining Star

At lunch, Aunt Jane made another announcement. "Today is Switch It Up Day. You must try something new! Maybe ride a new horse."

Avery grumbled.

"Missing one jumping lesson won't hurt you, Avery. Get out of your comfort zone!" said Jaelyn.

Aunt Jane continued. "Quickly decide what class to take. If you're vaulting, you'll need to change into yoga or sweat pants. Wear a double layer of socks, no boots."

She clapped her hands and we all scattered.

"I'll try dressage," said Carly.

"I'll come with you," said Kianna. "Where are you two going?"

At the same time, Gabriela and I both answered, "Vaulting."

Avery overheard. "Uh-oh. Could be double trouble."

"What does that mean?" asked Gabriela.

I pulled her toward the cabins.

After we changed, we walked behind the arena. Bree and Layla had Duke and Blue on longe lines in the middle of the circle. The circle was made from hay bales.

"I started vaulting last fall," said Aunt Jane. "Many of you have watched your friends enjoying it. Now it's your turn to try."

Aunt Jane ran her hand along Duke's belly. Then she rubbed Blue's neck. "Vaulting combines dance and gymnastics on the back of a moving horse. Anyone can vault. No fancy tumbles or jumps required. No gymnastics experience needed."

Layla spoke next. "Vaulting is the safest equestrian sport. It's so safe that helmets aren't allowed. They could get in the way and be dangerous if worn. So take them off."

Gabriela and I hadn't even brought ours. We knew Carly never needed one for her lessons.

"What do you think Layla and Bree are doing in the center of the circle?" asked Aunt Jane.

Gabriela's hand flew up. "They're longeurs. They control each horse's speed."

"Excellent," said Aunt Jane. "Vaulting takes teamwork. Bree, Layla, and I have been working together this summer. They let me focus so I can balance and feel safe."

She pointed to the barrel horses. "You've already practiced on those. Everyone knows the two basic moves."

Aunt Jane gave Duke a carrot and rubbed his nose. Then she mounted him and did a basic seat move. She held her arms out to the side and then raised them up to her ears.

"Don't forget to close your fingers, palms facing downward," she said. "Arch your fingers a little. Point your toes down and arch your feet." After that, she reviewed flag position.

Then it was our turn. Aunt Jane helped me mount Duke and Layla helped Gabriela get on Blue.

The basic seat move was easy.

"Go into flag position," said Aunt Jane.

I hopped up on my knees and extended my right leg straight out behind me.

"Nice," she said. "Hold your leg slightly above your head so it's parallel to the horse's spine."

As soon as I tried to move my leg, I wobbled.

"Careful," said Aunt Jane.

I looked over at Gabriela. She wasn't wobbling or shaking at all on Blue.

"Great leg extension, Gabriela," said Layla. "Make sure your other leg distributes the pressure through your shin and foot."

Gabriela extended her leg.

"You're a natural," said Layla.

Gabriela beamed.

Aunt Jane clicked her tongue. "Bring your fingers together, Dani. Palms down. Arch your fingers."

"Like this?" I asked.

Aunt Jane nodded. "Now make sure your right foot is arched and the bottom faces up."

But each time I tried to lift my foot up, I swayed back and forth.

I almost fell off. Twice!

When I looked over at Gabriela, she was standing on Blue. Standing! Blue snorted.

Layla gave Blue a sugar cube. "He trusts you, Gabriela."

Then Gabriela stood on one foot!

"Great balance. I think we have a star in you, Gabriela," said Layla.

Miss Perfect Pants strikes again!

"Look straight ahead, Dani," warned Aunt Jane. "If you keep looking over at Gabriela, you'll lose your balance."

So I tried again. This time, when I extended my leg, I didn't wobble. Not even a little.

"Bring yourself up to your knees while holding on to the surcingle," said Aunt Jane. "Then let go of it as

you slowly bring your body up to a complete stand. Keep your arms out to your sides and bend your knees a tiny bit. If you don't bend your knees, your legs will start to get shaky and you'll fall."

No matter how hard I tried to stand, I couldn't do it.

Aunt Jane held out her hand to me. "Spin my ring for luck."

So I turned the ring on her finger, but it didn't work.

Finally, I dismounted.

"Watch Gabriela," said Layla. "She's a pro at this."

Aunt Jane smiled at Layla. "Yes indeedy! A shining star."

I looked at the sky. If I saw a star, I'd make a wish and wish Gabriela away.

Chapter 7
Not So Brave

"How was vaulting?" asked Carly. "Isn't it the best thing ever?"

"I loved it," said Gabriela. "Aunt Jane called me a vaulting star!"

Carly narrowed her eyes. "Were you able to stand up?"

Gabriela nodded. "I stood up and balanced on Blue on my first try."

Carly looked surprised. "Wow! You *are* a star! What about you, Dani?"

"It was okay," I said.

"Okay?" said Carly. "Just *okay*?"

Now Carly rolled her eyes at me!

Rude, rude, rude! I sucked in my breath and starting timing.

"Vaulting's my *favorite* thing to do at Storm Cliff Stables," said Carly. "I can't believe you didn't *love* it."

"She didn't love it because she wasn't very good at it," said Gabriela. "She couldn't stand on Duke. Aunt Jane told her to dismount."

"That's not true! She didn't ask me to get off of Duke. I wanted to."

"Did you stand up?" asked Kianna.

I didn't say anything.

"Well?" said Gabriela. "Were you able to stand or not?"

Everyone stared at me.

"No," I finally whispered. "I didn't have enough time. If I had more time, I bet I could." Then I added, "I *know* I could."

Gabriela and Carly glanced at each other. They both had smirky faces.

"It's true!" I said.

"Take another lesson," said Carly. "You'll do it next time."

"There won't be a next time," I said. "I didn't like it."

Carly put her hands on her hips. "That's because you couldn't balance on Duke. If you were able to stand, you would have loved vaulting."

She was right.

"I finally did a handstand yesterday," said Carly. "While the horse was going around the circle!"

My mouth dropped open. So did Gabriela's.

Kianna gasped. "Are you serious? While Duke was moving?"

I didn't believe her.

Neither did Gabriela. "You're lying. You would have told us about it."

Carly crossed her heart. "I'm not lying. I wanted to keep it a secret. Aunt Jane said I could surprise everyone on Parents' Day."

We still didn't believe her.

"Want me to prove it?" she asked.

"How?" asked Gabriela.

Carly looked out the window. Her eyes lit up. "All the counselors have their daily meeting now with Aunt Jane, don't they?"

We nodded.

Carly smiled. It was a sneaky smile. The kind that means trouble.

"How about I show you?" she said. "We could go behind the arena right now. Aunt Jane has Duke and Blue tied up by the fence." She looked at Kianna. "You can be the longeur."

Kianna's eyes widened. "Not me. I've never done it before! Besides, I don't wanna get in trouble. We're not allowed to ride without permission."

She plopped down on the bunk. "If we break a rule, we could get kicked out of camp. My mama would sure be sore with me if that happened."

"But we're not officially riding a horse," said Carly. "We're vaulting. Way different. Besides, Aunt Jane's always telling us how safe vaulting is, isn't she?"

"But it's safe because Bree and Layla are the longeurs," said Gabriela. "We've never done that before." She looked at Kianna. "I'm not getting in trouble either."

I felt relieved. "If they don't go, we have no longeurs, so we can't go."

Carly tapped her chin. "I get it. You're afraid."

I stamped my foot. "I'm not afraid."

She turned to Kianna and Gabriela. "You're all afraid. A bunch of Pony Girl babies!"

Kianna pulled her legs up under her chin.

But Gabriela jumped up. "I'm not a baby. We just don't have a longeur."

"You can do it, Gabriela," said Carly. "You're good at everything. Aunt Jane and Layla said you're the vaulting star! You're the only one of us who can handle Blue. Remember? He lets you lead him, doesn't he?"

She nodded. "Just that one time."

"Then he'll let you do this, too," said Carly. "I just know it."

Gabriela chewed her bottom lip.

"Just think about it," said Carly. "You can practice on Blue, too. If you do, I bet you'll be the Vaulting Queen by next week!"

Gabriela's eyes lit up. "Okay. I'll go."

Carly clapped. "Great! Now that you're going, Dani will too. She'll get to stand up on Duke. Or Blue."

"Maybe both," said Gabriela.

Great.

Kianna spoke up. "Then I'll go, too. I'll make sure no one catches us because I really, really don't want to get in trouble." Then she sighed. "I wish I were as brave as you guys."

I wanted to tell Kianna that I wasn't brave at all. I was scared to stand on Duke. Really, really scared. And I was afraid of getting caught breaking the rules.

But I was even too afraid to tell her that.

Chapter 8
A Bad Idea

We rushed down to the arena.

"Make sure we're not being watched," said Carly.

We looked to the left. We looked to the right.

"There's no one around," I said.

"The coast is clear," Kianna agreed.

We rushed around to the back. Duke and Blue were exactly where Carly said they'd be.

I walked over to Duke. "Hiya, Duke. Can you keep a secret?"

He chortled.

"I'm pretty sure that means yes," said Carly.

"We're going to practice vaulting again," I said. Then when no one was looking, I whispered into his ear. "Stay nice and steady. I have to stand up on your back."

"Who's first?" asked Carly.

Kianna glanced around. "I'm not getting a good feeling about this."

"Too late now," said Carly.

Then she patted Duke's belly. "I'm going to show the Pony Girls that I can do a handstand on you."

Duke swatted his tail at a fly. Then he made a soft neighing sound.

"I'll be the longeur," said Gabriela. "I've watched Bree, Layla, and Aunt Jane do this. How hard can it be?"

She untied Duke to lead him to the circle. But Duke didn't move.

"Come on, Duke. Walk," she said.

But Duke just stood there.

Gabriela tried again. "We need you to walk now, Duke."

Duke refused to budge.

"What's wrong with him?" I asked.

Kianna twirled her finger around her ponytail. "I think Duke knows we're not supposed to be here. He doesn't want to get in trouble either."

"I'll go behind him and give him a little push," said Carly.

"No, no, no!" Gabriela and I said at the same time.

"Never walk behind a horse!" she said.

"He could kick you!" I finished. "What now?"

Kianna sighed. "There's nothing we can do. Let's just tie Duke back up and go."

Carly folded her arms over her chest. "No way. We didn't come just to see my handstand. We also came for Dani. She said that she could stand on Duke if she had more time. Now she has more time."

I gulped. "Is that what I said?" Suddenly Duke looked extra tall.

"That's what you said," said Gabriela. "Unless you were lying?"

"I wasn't lying," I said.

Carly clapped her hands. "Then we can have you stand on Duke now. You can get into a basic position and then move to flag. Then you ..."

"I know what to do," I said. "But how am I supposed to get on Duke?"

Everyone looked around. There weren't any stools. No Aunt Jane or Layla to help us.

Carly squatted and cupped her hands. "I'll help you."

But as soon as I put my foot in Carly's cupped hands, her hands broke apart.

So we tried again. And again.

"Let me try," said Gabriela.

But the same thing happened.

"Let me get Blue," said Gabriela. "Maybe he'll bring us luck."

"No," said Kianna. "We're not supposed to be here. That's why nothing's working." She scanned the area. "Let's get out of here before we get caught."

That was the best idea I'd heard all day!

But it was too late.

We were caught!

"What are you girls doing here?" called Avery. She stomped over to us. Esha was with her.

Esha looked around. "You're in big, big trouble! You're not allowed to be with a horse without an adult. Where's Layla? Where's Aunt Jane?"

Avery's face was red. She looked mad. Madder than mad. "In a meeting, that's where."

Esha grabbed the lead rope. "Bree needs Duke. That's why we came. We never thought we'd find Pony Girls here."

Esha looked at Avery. "And Aunt Jane calls *me* her Wild Child?"

"Start talking," said Avery.

So we spilled the beans.

"I'm glad Duke refused to move," said Avery. "You could have gotten hurt! And just because Blue let you lead him once, doesn't mean he'd listen to you today. He gets cranky."

She pointed to the bales of hay. "Kianna and Carly, go sit over there."

Then she told us to sit by the fence.

"You girls are cousins. But you spend all your time being jealous of each other. You barely know each other! And it seems like you don't *want* to get to know each other."

"That's not true at all," said Gabriela.

Avery put her finger up to her lip. "You don't know how lucky you both are that you have cousins. I don't have any."

"None?" I asked.

"Nope. But if I did, I wouldn't be acting like a brat. I'd be making memories. Sharing secrets. Planning sleepovers."

Gabriela started to cry.

Then I cried.

"I'm sorry," said Gabriela. "I have been bratty."

I wiped my nose with my hand. "Me too."

But we weren't the only ones crying.

When we looked over at Kianna and Carly, they were hugging Aunt Jane. She was crying harder than we were!

We rushed over to them.

"I doubt we can find it, Aunt Jane," said Layla, who had walked up, too. "It's a big lake. The water's murky."

Aunt Jane wiped her eyes. "That lucky ring was my grandmother's. It means the world to me."

Aunt Jane took a deep breath. "I wish I hadn't ended our meeting early. It was just so hot I thought a quick dip before afternoon activities would be perfect. But as soon as I dove in, I felt it slip off of my finger."

Aunt Jane covered her eyes with her hands. "There wasn't anything I could do. I'm just heartbroken."

Kianna hugged Aunt Jane. "Mama would say we just need a plan."

"Yeah. We can at least *try* to find it in that murky water," I said.

Gabriela and Carly agreed. Finally, Layla and Aunt Jane did too.

We rushed down to the lake and swam out to the float.

"I dove in right here," said Aunt Jane. "But it could be anywhere. I tried diving down, but I couldn't go down very far."

Layla turned to Gabriela. "You're the best swimmer here. You should look for it."

So Gabriela dove in. But she just kept swimming back and forth.

"You have to dive," said Carly. "It's probably all the way on the bottom."

Gabriela tried but popped back up quickly. "I can't get to the bottom." She climbed back up on the float.

"Thanks for trying," said Aunt Jane. "It could have floated off in any direction. I'm sure it's gone for good. It's probably already buried in the soft sand down there."

"There's only one person who can find it, Aunt Jane," said Gabriela.

"Who?" asked Aunt Jane.

"Yeah," I said. "Who?"

Gabriela pointed to me. "You."

I took a step back. "Me?"

"Yes, you. You're the only one who can hold her breath underwater long enough."

"You're the best sea monkey," said Kianna. She turned to Aunt Jane. "Dani is the Hold Your Breath Queen."

Gabriela nodded. "And the Ring Dive Queen! She can find anything down there."

"But this ring is so tiny," I said. "I don't know if I can hold my breath that long."

"You can," said Gabriela. "My mom told me that you swim under the waterfalls in Costa Rica and hold your breath like a fish. She said you want to be like that man in Brazil!"

"What man in Brazil?" said Layla.

"The man who can hold his breath for eleven minutes underwater," said Gabriela. "He holds the world record."

"Your mom told you that?" I asked. "How did she know?"

Gabriela nodded. "Abuela told my mom and my mom told me."

That made me happy.

I looked at Aunt Jane. "I can hold my breath for over a minute. I practice all the time."

"More than a minute!" said Aunt Jane. "I'm not sure that's safe."

Layla sat on the float. "She does it all the time. I've timed her."

Before Aunt Jane could stop me, I dove into the water and easily skimmed the bottom of the lake. I felt leaves and rocks. I swam back to the surface. "Nothing so far."

I dove back down again. This time, I slowly pushed my hands along the bottom of the lake. When I came up, Aunt Jane looked worried. "You were under there for almost a minute. It's too dangerous."

"I'm not even out of breath," I said.

I dove back down again. When I came up, I pumped my fist in the air. "I found something."

Aunt Jane clasped her hands together. "My ring?"

"Nope." I held up a pair of green goggles and tossed them to Kianna.

That's when I noticed the trees swaying. "It's windy. The wind is blowing that way, Aunt Jane. I'm going to look over there."

Gabriela called, "Smart idea!"

Aunt Jane shook her head. "It's no use. The ring is gone. It could be a hundred feet in either direction by now. Or caught in a patch of weeds."

But it wasn't a hundred feet away. When I dove down again, I saw something sparkle in the sand. I

swam toward it and scooped it up. Then I swam back to the surface.

I swam over to Aunt Jane. She sat on the edge of the float. She looked like she was going to cry again.

Please let this be Aunt Jane's ring.

"I found something, Aunt Jane." I lifted my hand out of the water and held up the ring.

"You found it!" called Aunt Jane.

Kianna, Carly, and Gabriela jumped into the water and jumped on me. I almost dropped the ring!

"Amazing," said Layla. "You did it, Dani!"

"You're the only one who could have found it, Dive Queen!" said Gabriela.

Chapter 10
Pack Your Bags

Aunt Jane made a fuss over me at the campfire. She let me have as many s'mores as I wanted. Then she let me pick the games we played and choose the songs we sang. I even got to assign the skits for the night. After the skits, she made a speech and thanked me all over again.

"Once again, the girls at Storm Cliff Stables pulled together to help someone out. Today that someone was me.

"I lost a special ring in the lake today. I thought it was gone forever. But a Pony Girl came to the rescue. Dani Cruz kept diving down to the bottom of the lake until she found it."

Some girls started to clap, but Aunt Jane held up her hand.

"I'm always impressed with how well we come together to help each other. Today was a perfect example. Dani saved the day. Let's give her a huge round of applause."

The girls clapped so loud and for so long that I covered my ears.

Then Aunt Jane spoke again. "To celebrate the spirit of not only Dani's willingness to help out, but for every one of you who mucks out stalls, picks up trash on the trails, and takes time to visit the animals, I salute you. Let's sing our camp song."

We sang it three times!

Aunt Jane was in such a good mood that she let us make popcorn over the fire. Then she asked the older girls to bring some of the horses to the campfire. She even extended the campfire by forty-five minutes.

Avery and Esha came up to me.

"You're brave," said Esha. "There's no way I'd ever want to crawl on the bottom of that lake. There's probably snakes slitherin' down there."

"She's from Costa Rica. She's used to snakes," said Gabriela. "And did you know she's a lepidopterist?"

"A what?" asked Esha.

"A butterfly expert," said Gabriela. "She's the Butterfly Queen, you know. It's official. My abuela said so."

Avery bowed and said, "All hail the Butterfly Queen."

When Esha and Avery left to make popcorn, Gabriela sat on a log. I plopped down next to her.

"I have to tell you something," Gabriela said. "Something not so nice."

"What?" I asked. My heart was pounding.

"I came to camp not liking you," she said. "Avery was right. I was jealous. You know all the cousins. I don't. You know everything about

Costa Rica. I don't. You're Abuela's favorite granddaughter. I'm not."

"That's not true! She just doesn't know you," I said. "Why don't you ever visit?"

"My parents don't have time to take me. They said I can go but I won't fly alone."

"Come with us!" I said. "We'll go together!"

"You wouldn't mind?" she asked.

I hugged her. "Mind? I'd love it! That's what cousins do for each other."

"But before we plan our trip, I have something to tell you," I said. "I've been jealous of you, too. You're so smart. You know how to do everything! You can even do french braids. But you're the reason I even know about Storm Cliff Stables!"

Gabriela hugged me. "My teacher would call us two silly gooses."

We both laughed.

"I'm glad I'm getting to know you, Dani. You're my BFF *and* my BCF."

"Best Cousins Forever?" I asked.

"Yep! Unless . . ."

"Unless what?" I asked.

"Unless I meet a nicer one in Costa Rica!" We had a giggle fit.

Just then, Aunt Jane walked by. We scooted over and let her sit next to us.

Gabriela said, "Do we *have* to stay here for an extra forty-five minutes?"

Aunt Jane raised her eyebrows. "You don't want to stay here?"

"It's not that I don't want to," she said. "It's just that I need to make another BFF frame. But this time, mine's going to say BCF."

Aunt Jane looked confused. "BCF?"

I squeezed Gabriela tight. "Best Cousins Forever."

"I think we can arrange that," said Aunt Jane. Then she yawned.

"Are you plum tuckered out, Aunt Jane?" asked Gabriela.

"I sure am. I still need that vacation."

Gabriela put her head on my shoulder. "Have you ever thought about going to Costa Rica? It's the most beautiful place on Earth, you know."